Thanks to my sons, Ellis and Lino.
Thanks to Thalie for her continued support and patience in the last weeks of getting this book ready. A big thanks to Alec Longstreth, my Jedi Master of colour!

MAX DE RADIGUÈS

STIG & TILDE

THE LOSER SQUAD

NOBROW

London | New York

Tysla!
We're finally here!
I can't wait to have a proper shower!
And eat frozen pizzas!
To sleep in clean sheets that smell of fabric conditioner-
and are treated against mosquitos!
We can listen to music...
...and go on the internet!
Do you think mum and dad are gonna be mad at us?
Probably...
But they'll be glad that we're ok, right?
And we've still got two weeks before coming back. That will give them some time to calm down.
Yeah...
Hey look, someone's coming to greet us!

They won't believe their eyes that we're here.
And when we tell them all that we've been through...
Hmm... I don't think they saw us...
Isn't that your friend? The one who loves magic?
What?
Yoni?
YOOONIII!!
Hey!
WOOHOO!
?
Hello my friend! Ahh, it's so good to see you!
Stig?! Tilde?!
What are you guys doing here?!

Hehe...
You're not gonna believe it, but...
...we've actually been –
I thought you left ages ago.
Left?!
Well yeah, like all the others.
We just got here, what are you talking about?
Huh?
You weren't here when...
YOOONI
Crap!
They're already here!
YOOONI

Well well Yoni... who are your new friends?
What's your problem, Falco?
You know that guy?
He was in my ballet class.
Ho ho!
My parents made me!
Yeah, yeah, sure.
Don't get involved in this, Tilde. It's between me and this thief, Yoni.
Knut!
Hey!
My bag!
Shut up, Yoni.
All this for two packets of biscuits and a water bottle?
The Loser Squad is getting more and more pathetic...
Knut, take them.

WHOAH, WHOAH, WHOAH! Wait!
Hmm?
I don't get it? How could Yoni be stealing when everything belongs to everyone on this island?
Pfff...
Where have you been these past two weeks?
Everything belongs to me, and I decide who I wanna share it with.
You and Yoni for example, you're not allowed to have anything.
Your sister however...
She...
She could have everything.
BAM
Knut!
AAAAH
Grab your friend and get the hell out of here!
Yeah!

Haha! I can't believe it! Did you see how they ran away?!
This way.
Huh... Isn't the campsite on the other side?
We're not going there.
Didn't you hear Falco? We're not welcome at the campsite.
Why did you think we'd left? Did no one even notice that we never arrived?
Never arrived?
It was complete mayhem here, from the very first day...

Falco made himself chief, on the grounds that his dad is gonna buy the island from the council.
He threw people out of the camp.
The criteria were things like: I don't like you, I don't like your face, you're too small...
And even nastier things... like he said to Raja.
"You already have Ramadan, Kulku is for us! Go home!"
Really?
Falco said THAT!
Yeah, things went downhill from there. People were constantly fighting, for days...
Then Knut broke a girl's arm. He didn't mean to, but... it happened.
A lot of people left the island.
The others were afraid to confront Falco.
Now, his clique rules the official camp and then there's us.
Us?
Yeah, the Wolves Club!

Or the Loser Squad, as they like to call us.
Wow!
What is this place?
It's the island's first campsite, before they built a new one in the 70s.
I've heard a woman and a wolf built the first house.
Come!
Hey, Yoni's back!
YONI!

So?
Mission accomplished!
Yay! Well done, Yoni!
Awesome!
Your mission?!
Your mission was to get two packets of biscuits and water?
Who are they?
Stig and his sister Tilde.
Hi!
They've just arrived. They're with us now.
My mission wasn't the biscuits, I –

Guess who just carried out Tysla's greatest mission?
THE WOLVES CLUB!
Great!
Woo!
Yeah!
You were just a diversion then!
Right?
Exactly!
We've got everything!
Everything!
Flour, eggs, bacon...
Milk, biscuits, chocolate...
Fruit?
Crisps, soda...
We're sorted!
We even thought of you, Naïa!
We found an old walkman with batteries and an old cassette, Now! Vol. 2!
Hehe.
Ah! Cool! I don't even care what it is, as long as it's music!
Was it ok, Yoni?
Yep.

Thanks to these two!
Who are these two?
TILDE!
STIG!
My friends!
Haha! Hi Ada...
They saved me from Falco and Knut. You should have seen it!
Falco was chatting up Tilde when...
KISS
KISS
BAM! She swung her knee right into his nuts!
PAK
And two seconds later, KA-CHING! They whipped out a bow and an axe from their bags!
Real ninjas!
Knut ran away with Falco in his arms! Ha ha!
I think our club has just found two new Wolves!
Yeah!
Yay!
CLAP
CLAP
CLAP
CLAP

Let me introduce you...
Alwin
Naïa
Mariell
Edi
Ole
Hey!
Hatem
Rikke
Raja
You know Yoni.
And I!
Ok, we need to put all this away...
I'll start preparing dinner.
I'll help you!
Ok.
Alwin and the new girl, go look for firewood.
Rikke and Hatem, you guys take care of the water.
As for the rest, count me out!
Ole, I doubt they'll be coming but would you mind guarding the camp?
No problems, I'll be back at sundown.
Thanks.

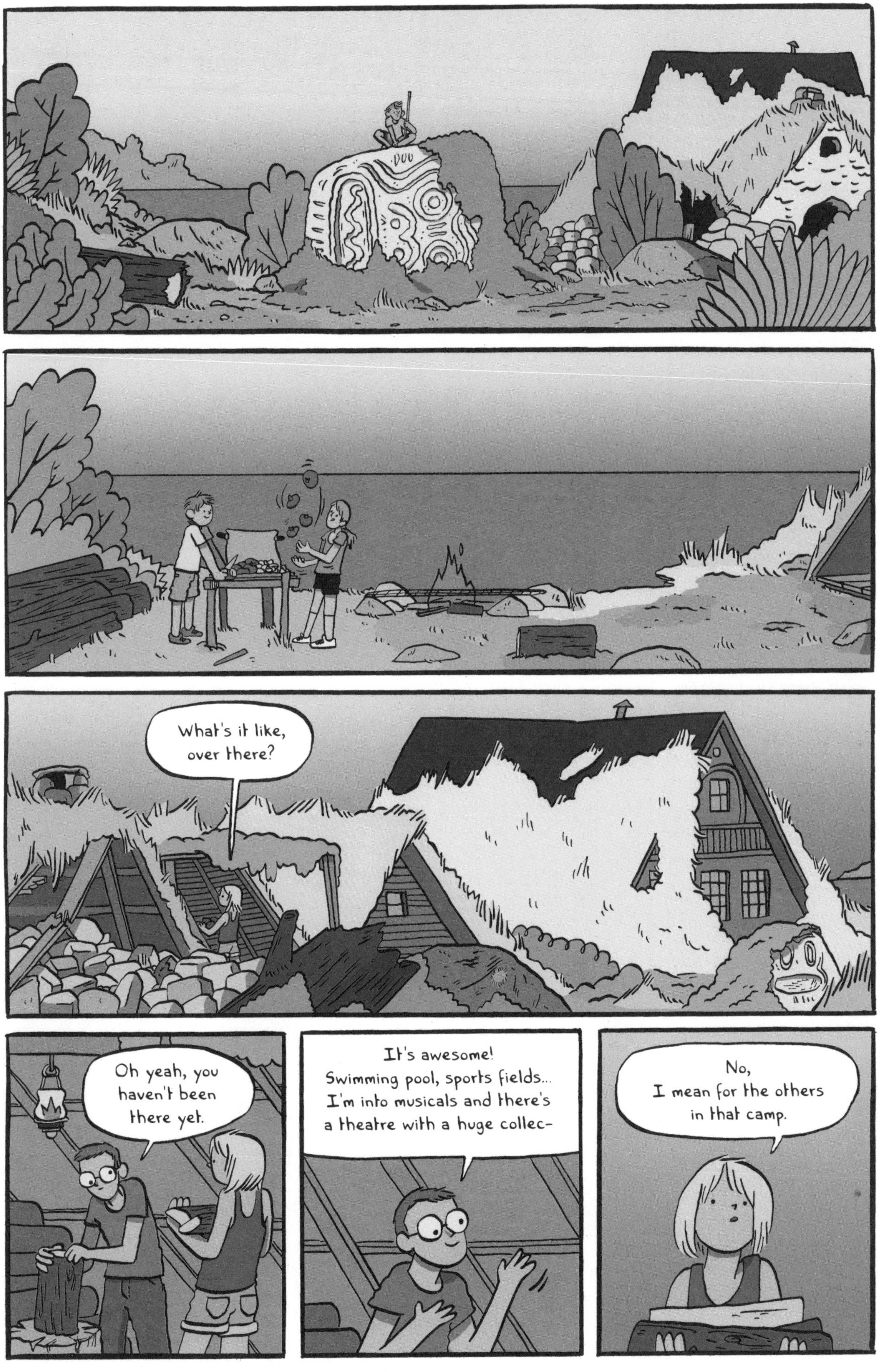

What's it like, over there?
Oh yeah, you haven't been there yet.
It's awesome! Swimming pool, sports fields... I'm into musicals and there's a theatre with a huge collec-
No, I mean for the others in that camp.

Ah... hmm.
They're fine... Honestly, it's not that bad.
There are about 60 people there...
...and around fifteen are with Falco.
THWACK
But if you're not on Falco's radar, it's actually pretty cool.
Paradise even!
You know, a lot of them help us by leaving tools and food just outside the camp.
But why do they tolerate Falco?
They're just trying not to get banned.
THWACK
Banned?!
Yeah, there are a few that he didn't get rid of at the beginning but who he no longer wants there.
Take Ada for example, she arrived here just a few days ago.
Really?
She was there until Falco tried to make a move on her...
Yeah, the typical unwanted advances of a creep!

He banned you because you refused to go out with him?
Worse than that...
BRLRL
He banned me cause I told him I like girls!
They locked me up in the gym all night. The next day, I went straight to my boat.
TCHAF TCHAF
I knew about the club so I decided to sail around the island and come here.
They locked you up all night?
They always do that.
By the way, there was a girl in the gym when we were there this afternoon.
I wonder if you know her...
What? Who is it?
Can you put this on the fire, Stig?
Yep.
Her name sounds like that girl from Harry Potter... Hermimonie or something?
Hermine?!
I think so.
We must get her out!
Leave it, after what we did this afternoon they'll be mega on edge.
But...
She's right, Tilde.
If she wants to join us, she'll find us. There's nothing we can do for her.
But...
MEAL'S READY IN 15 MINUTES!!!
But...

ARGH!
BOO!
Are you ok, Tilde?
ARGH! Ish hot!

Stig!
Stig!
Wake up!
Mmh...
What's going on?
We must find Hermine!
What?! Are you nuts?! Didn't you hear what the others said?!
Quiet, you're going to wake everyone up.
Come on... Let's go outside.
Pleeeaase!
Urgh...
Ok, let's do it...
Wait!
You're gonna need equipment and a guide.

Wow!
These outfits are so cool
Yeah, we got a bunch of stuff from the camp. A real goldmine!
Swift! Agile! Creeping like a cat...
Known to the police as 'The Feline', an unparallelled thief...
...it's none other than Stig!
Hop
The Feline roll!
Woo!
Whoooo...
Can we go now, The Feline?
Hmph...
We're getting close. No flashlights from this point.

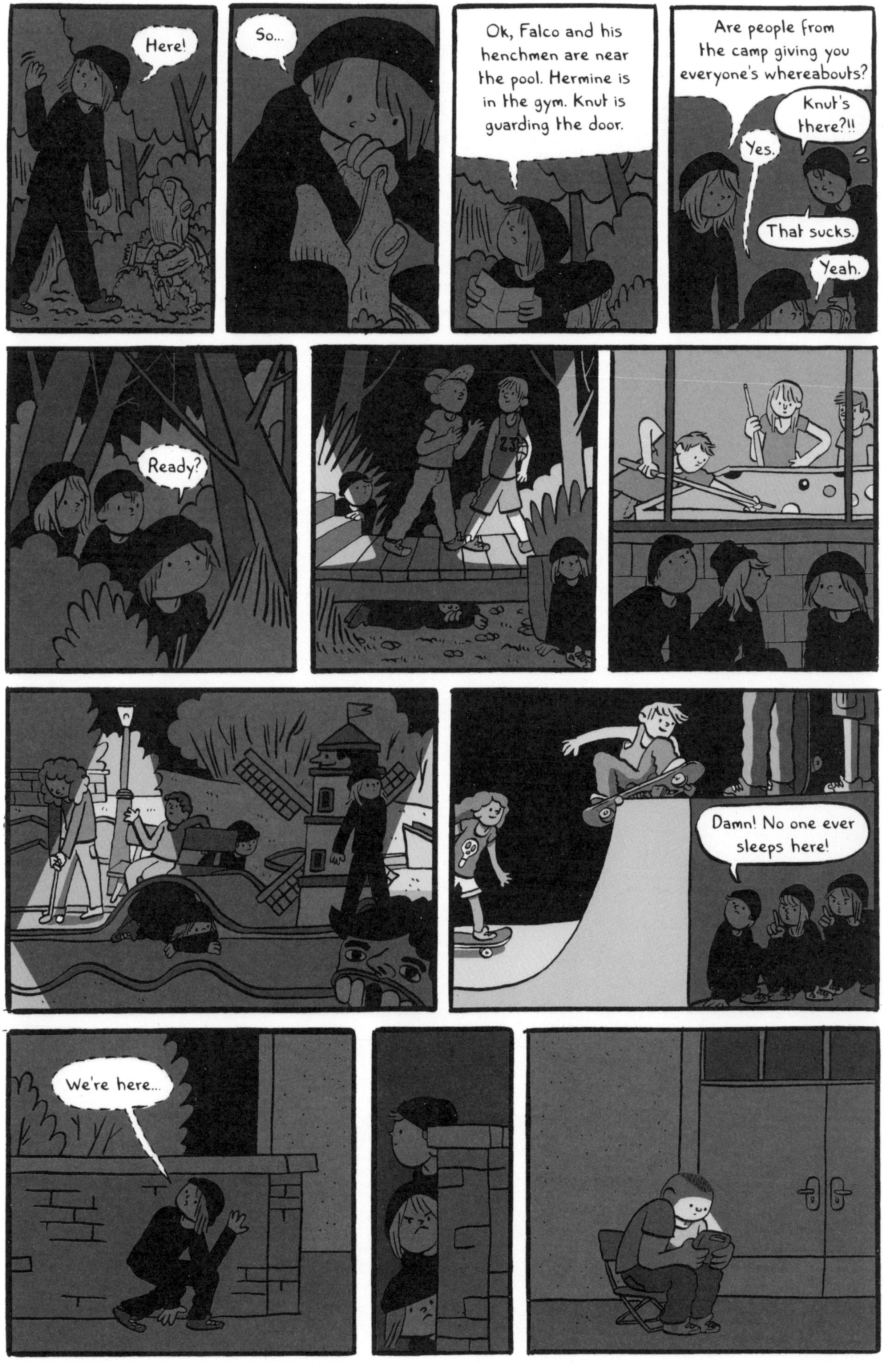
Here!
So...
Ok, Falco and his henchmen are near the pool. Hermine is in the gym. Knut is guarding the door.
Are people from the camp giving you everyone's whereabouts?
Yes.
Knut's there?!!
That sucks.
Yeah.
Ready?
Damn! No one ever sleeps here!
We're here...

You can get in through the roof.
Ok.
Ok.
There!
Oh man. It's super high!
Nah, it's not...
Hermine! It's Tilde! Put a mattress under us if you can!
Very high...
Tilde?

Come on! Boys first!
What?!
No, no! You go, it's your friend!
Come on, be strong, The Feline...
Come on! Hop!
ARGH
BWOOOOOOUF!
Are you ok?
Yeah, yeah no worries! Easy peasy!

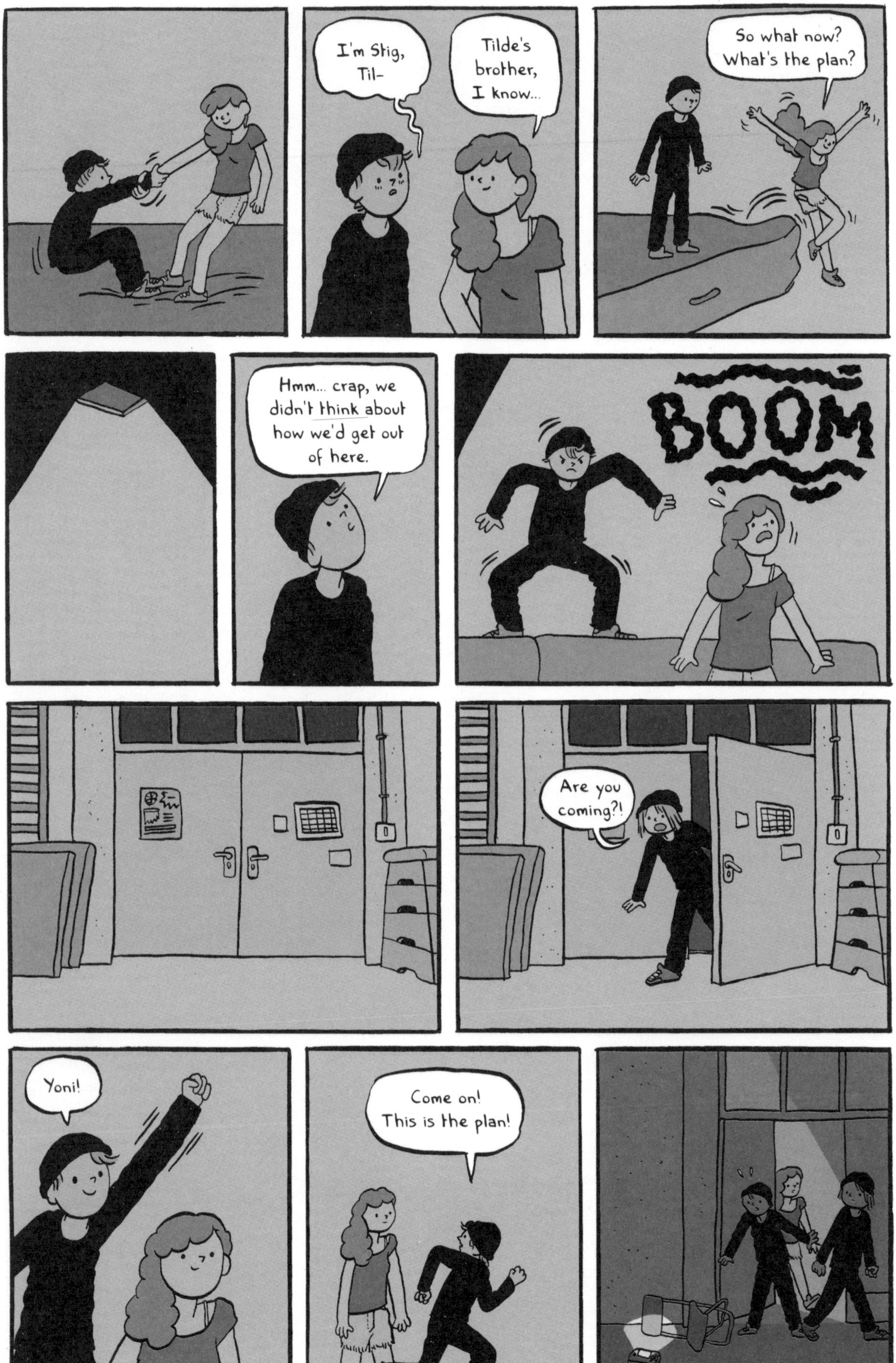
I'm Stig, Til-
Tilde's brother, I know...
So what now? What's the plan?
Hmm... crap, we didn't think about how we'd get out of here.
BOOM
Are you coming?!
Yoni!
Come on! This is the plan!

What happened to Knut?
Tilde knocked him out.
At least she tried to...
RUUUUN!
Hey.
MINI-GOLF MAXI-FUN

Pffft! Ha ha!
Ha ha ha!
Are you ok?
What are these outfits?
Ha ha!
You should have seen Knut's face when he saw us!
Haha! Yeah, "if only I could run with these big muscly legs"...
Ha!
I think we lost "big legs". We're in the clear now.
PFRRFF!
Ha ha!
Ha ha!
Ha ha!
Thanks for getting me out of there!
You're welcome.
Shall we head back?

Wake up!
Hmm
RAJA?!
I thought we agreed not to go and free her!
Err... but, no one saw us! We were very... err... discreet!
Ha!
Tssk... All this for her.

What did Ada mean?
Do you know each other?
No.
But...
it's probably because I...
I was Falco's girlfriend.
WHAT?!
I know...
He was into me and...
Great! Cause he's
obviously not the type
to be into just anybody.
How lucky
you were!
I know... he's trash. He
treats people like garbage,
and girls even more so.
But I was happy being
the centre of attention... like
the queen of the island.
Gross, Hermine!
You always hang out
with the world's biggest
scumbags!
Yeah...
Maybe we get
what we deserve.

Pff... No one deserves Falco.
You could have anyone you want... Why don't you pick nice guys?
Like my brother or... Yoni?
Your brother?! I saw how he was looking at Ada.
Hm. You're right.
But he falls in love with any girl that smiles at him...
It was just an example.
Yeah. Falco was openly flirting with lots of other girls...
And he would put his hands everywhere, even when I pushed him away.
I couldn't take it any more. I tried to break up with him...
So he banned me.
What a filth bucket creepazoid!
Yeah, well... You're next on his list.
Ha! My ex was a psycho poltergeist so Falco doesn't impress me...
WHAT?!

And then, Stig cut my hair with his axe! I was free!
PAM
Ouch!
Well, between this lumberjack haircut and death, I'd definitely choose the hair!
We got to the limit of his territory, and he watched us leave...
That's a crazy story!
See, you're not the only one who hangs out with goons...
Yeah we're almost even.
Well, it's not us. It's guys who are all weasels!
Ha! Exactly!
Well, all except you, Yoni!
YONI!
YONI! YONI! YONI! YONI! YONI!

Ah there you are! Where have you been?
Listen Ada, I want to apologise.
You were banned cause you stood up to Falco and you knew how to say no.
I did too, it just took me longer to figure out than you.
I may not be as strong or as smart as you are...
But I know as well as you that he's a creep. Ultimately, you did better than me.
Ok, now this is all done, I'm going to have a look at the camp. Tilde, you wanna come with me?

Huh, isn't the camp that way?
We're not going to our camp, we're going to their camp!
Ah...
I'm sure you didn't see much during last night's raid...
Wait... Are we cool, Raja? Are you mad at me for getting Hermine?
Are you kidding?
I'm happy that I'm not the only one who wants to shake things up a bit!
If it was down to me, we would have beaten the shit out of Faleu and his gang a long time ago.
One good old fight, and then we could call it a night.

I agree... but we're just a bunch of outcasts. I'm not sure we could compete.
Yeah, but us Wolves have tougher skin than they do.
And if something were to change, I'm sure a lot of people from the camp would join us.
Ha, I wouldn't count on that too much...
They've seen loads of people get banned, but they never lifted a finger!
They're too attached to their cushy lives now.
No way!
"What a tough day, the pool was too cold, I had to queue for the showers...
There's no chilli oil left for my pizza, a fly fell in my coke...
Someone got banned?! I hope I get her breakfast tomorrow..."
Haha, you're harsh...
Oh!

Pretty great, huh?
Here, take the binoculars and enjoy the view...
Wow, a swimming pool!
Everyone's got their own bedroom?
There's even a skatepark! I've always wanted to learn...
Ooooh...
Wow!
Try and spot Falco and his guys.

Wait...That's Mariell!
What?!
And she's going to Falco?
What?!
Give me those!
She followed him into a building...
Well, we'll wait for her then...!

After two weeks of living in the wild this looks like heaven.
Heaven?! Personally, I think it's more like a fascist dictatorship.
Look at them. Having fun like everything's normal.
Well, a lot of them are rebelling. Quite a few are helping you, aren't they?
If we were in Harry Potter, Falco would be in Slytherin and we'd be in Gryffindor!
And for the ultimate fight, all the other houses would join us!
I haven't read Harry Potter.
What? You've gotta be kidding me!
Wait, I think she's coming out...
That's her. Come on, let's go!

I can't believe you've never read Harry Potter!
What will we do when we catch her?
FRRRRRR
I don't know, we'll see when we get her.
She can stay with them for all I care.
Well that's not very Gryffindor...
What?
Get ready...
Mmh.
AAAAH!
Oh, it's you! You scared the hell out of me! Are you ok?
No, we're not ok, Mariell.

But what have I –
We saw you with Falco!
Oh.
But it's nothing, nothing at all...
...believe me...
Ok.
I have no patience, Mariell!
ARGH
Whoa, whoa. Whoah! Wait!
Ok, ok, I went to see Falco to tell him Tilde was the one who released Hermine.
Why?
I...
I...
I don't want you to steal Yoni from me!
What?!
I only joined the Wolves Club because of Yoni. I've seen how you look at him!
What?! That's not true! I don't give a damn about Yoni.
And what else did you tell Falco?
He asked lots of questions about Tilde. I told him the story about her ex the poltergeist.
He sounded super excited, asking for all the details...

Is that it?
Yes! I swear, I swear!
Uh?
Aren't you guys mad at me?
Honestly Mariell, we couldn't care less. I kissed a ghost. So what, why does it matter?
Can I come with you then?
Choose your side, Mariell!
I'm with Yoni! I mean...
...the Wolves.
Then you'll come with us.
Will you tell the others?
Not even Yoni.

Where have you been?
Nowhere.
What's going on?
Falco is leaving the island!
What?!
Alone?
To go where ???
We don't know. He took a boat and went away.
Towards town?
No, the opposite way.
Huh, guys...

KNUT!
What the hell does he want?
I don't know, but we'll stop him.
Stay where you are!
What do you want?
Tomorrow, 6pm. Here!!!
We settle this once and for all. The losers leave the island!
What should we say?
Uhh...
No blades, spikes or weapons!
Blades?
What?!
Sticks and fists! Ok! See you tomorrow, Losers... Enjoy your last night here!

What should we do then?
...
Mmh.
Hmm...
Huh...
...
I know! I'll ask the wolves to come and help us!
Damn, it looks like there are no wolves on this island.
Ok.
TAP
TAP
Ada and Hermine, you know them best. I want a list of all their strengths and weaknesses.
Alwin and Naïa, the battle field...
Try and work out how we can use the field to our advantage.
We're on it!

Edi, find us what we need to defend ourselves.
I'll come with you.
Hatem, you...
Rikke and I will make a meal for champions! We'll need some strength!
Huh... ok.
I have a brilliant idea, can I go with Yoni?
Now?
Well... ok...
Wait, I'm coming with you!
That's only us left, then...
Yep!
Are you ok, Raja?
Pff, I have no idea what I'm doing!
You were perfect!
Look, they've all got something to do. They've almost forgotten why they are doing all of this.

Before we came here, Tilde and I were on an island full of masks carved out of wood. It was so creepy!
BAM! We've made one for everyone! These will terrify our enemies!
Wanna try them on?
Ha ha! Perfect!
Scary! Ok, we've got 3 hours left before they arrive, we-
Oh no...

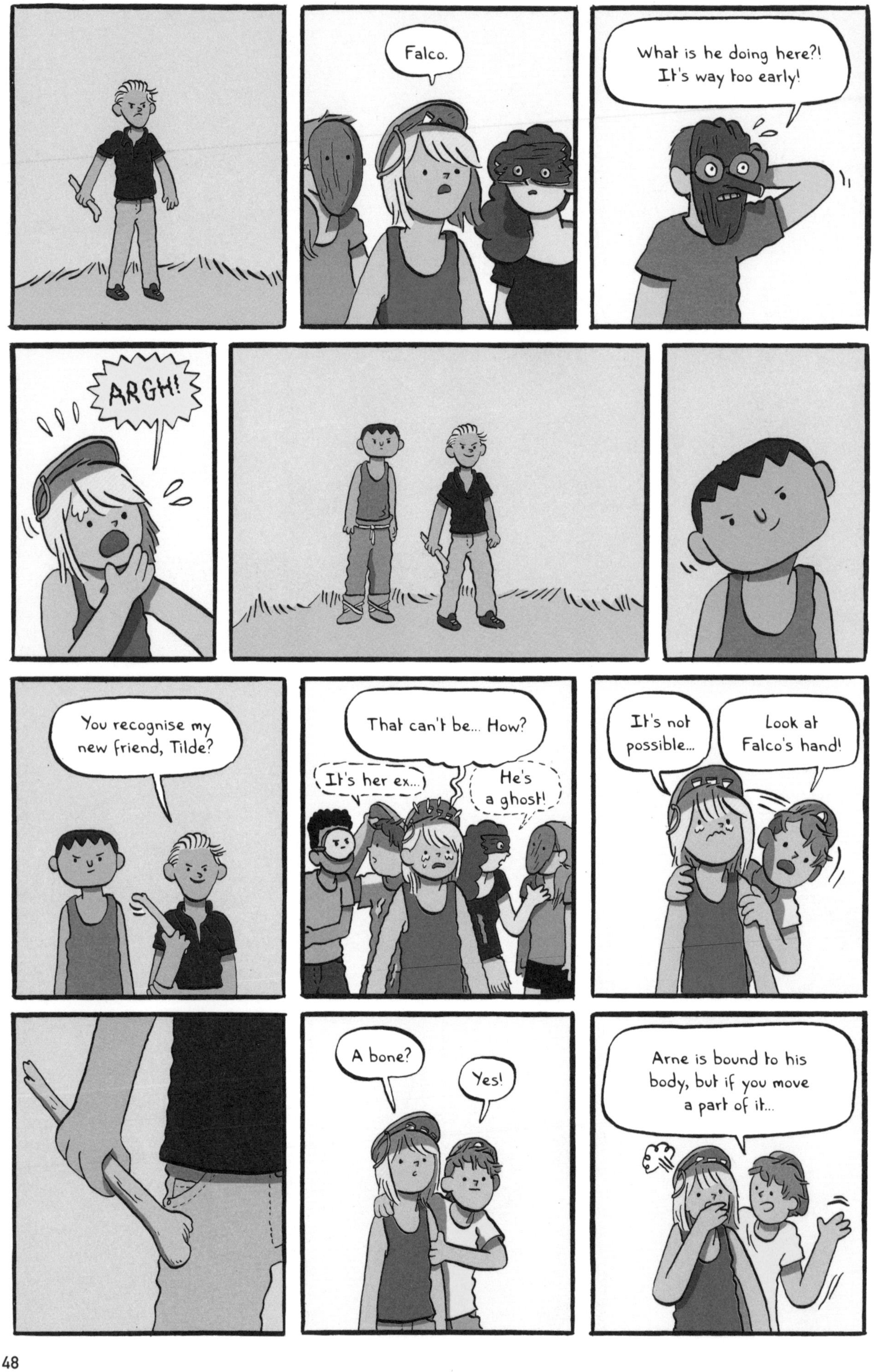

Falco.
What is he doing here?! It's way too early!
ARGH!
You recognise my new friend, Tilde?
That can't be... How?
It's her ex...
He's a ghost!
It's not possible...
Look at Falco's hand!
A bone?
Yes!
Arne is bound to his body, but if you move a part of it...

Damn!
Falco, his henchmen, and a poltergeist? We're dead!
You know Tilde, I had a long discussion with our mutual friend...
And I'm taking you off my list. I'll leave you to Arne.
I'll be content with Ada or Hermine...
The only list I'm on is a list of people who are gonna kick your ass!
Ha ha! Oh Tilde. I'll miss you once you leave the island with Arne.
Let's be honest, you have no chance!
He's right. We'd better leave now.
What do we do?
It's not over yet.
?

The others from the camp? How?
I went to see them last night.
Guys... what do we do? We can't kick everyone off the island...
Why not?
23
Do you really think a few more Losers will make a difference?!
We're going to smash you!

Wow!
ARGH!
Oh!
ARGH!
A wolf!
A wolf!
A wolf!
Waah! I'm so happy to see you little one!
I knew I could talk to wolves.
For the Wolves Club!

Stig, we must destroy that bone!
I'm on it...

RAAH!
My turn!
ARF
Ha!
It's over...
Matilda...
Matilda!

GRRRR
You and your friends have ten minutes to leave the island.
After that, I release my wolves.
Out of my way! Let me go!
YEAH!
Get lost, Falco!
How did you know that we needed help?
Last night, my white wolf Maïa ran to the water and started swimming away...
No one else could have called her except you.

Matilda?
Say bye to Tilde, Arne.
I'll show you where I live.
I think we need to talk...
And we both need company.
Are you sure about this?
Don't worry about me, I've seen worse than a broken-hearted poltergeist.
Farewell, Tilde.
Huh... What just happened?
Arne and Matilda have an old score to settle. But as for us...
We won!
Awesome.

SLIIIII IIIIIDE

Say it ain't
My love is
KiPS
KiPS
Just a sec...
Ok.

Are you ok, Tilde?
Yeah... we got what we wanted, right? Pizzas, a swimming pool...
But you'd like to explore the other islands, right?
After all we've still got a few days left before heading back home...
... and we've got plenty of boats!

ABOUT THE AUTHOR

Max de Radiguès is a Belgian cartoonist and publisher for L'employé Du Moi and Sarbacane. His work is for both adults and children, alike.

In September 2009, he was invited for a one year residency at the prestigious Center for Cartoon Studies in White River Junction, USA. He recounted this year in his book *Meanwhile In White River Junction*, which was part of the official selection for the 2012 Angoulême International Comics Festival. In 2018, Max de Radiguès received the College prize at the Angoulême festival and the Polar SNCF prize for his graphic novel *Bastard* (Fantagraphics). He currently lives in Brussels, Belgium.

IF YOU MISSED THE FIRST TWO STIG & TILDE ADVENTURES THEN CHECK OUT:

STIG & TILDE
VANISHER'S ISLAND

STIG & TILDE
LEADER OF THE PACK

First published in English in 2020 by Nobrow Ltd.
27 Westgate Street, London E8 3RL.

Published in agreement with Éditions Sarbacane through Sylvain Coissard Agency.

Text and illustrations by Max de Radiguès.

Translation by Marie Bédrune.

1 3 5 7 9 10 8 6 4 2

Published in the US by Nobrow (US) Inc.
Printed in Poland on FSC® certified paper.

MIX
Paper from
responsible sources
FSC
www.fsc.org
FSC® C001693

ISBN: 978-1-910620-66-3
www.nobrow.net